ICE HOUSE SKETCHES

FICTION

BY

ROBERT PHILLIPS

Texas Review Press
Huntsville, Texas

FIRST EDITION, 2011
Requests for permission to reproduce material from this work
should be sent to:

> Permissions
> Texas Review Press
> English Department
> Sam Houston State University
> Huntsville, TX 77341-2146

Acknowledgements:

Some sections of this work appeared originally in *Stone Canoe: A
    Journal of Arts and Ideas from Upstate New York.*
The "Millie" episode is from an anecdote by Leon Hale.
"Blabbermouth" is based upon an anecdote in Sherwood Anderson's
    Memoirs.

Poems on pages 47,64 & 68 are by Farrell Dyde (with permission).

Thanks to David Monroe and Farrell Dyde for word processing.

Thanks to the University of Houston for a grant that gave me time to
    write some of this book.

Thanks to my wife Judith, who endured (like Dilsey) while I wrote these
    pieces.

Elements of cover graphic taken from Russell Lee's photograph of a
Harlingen, Texas, ice house, 1939. Cover design by Virginia Houk.

**Note: This is a work of fiction. Any resemblance to persons or places is
purely coincidental.**

Library of Congress Cataloging-in-Publication Data

Phillips, Robert S.
  Ice house sketches / Robert Phillips. -- 1st ed.
     p. cm.
  ISBN 978-1-933896-65-6 (pbk. : alk. paper)
  1. Bars (Drinking establishments)--Texas--Fiction. 2. Texas--
Fiction. I. Title.
  PS3566.H5I25 2011
  813'.54--dc22

                              2011007981

To John T. Irwin,
poet, professor, editor and Houston boy

CONTENTS

ON THE LATE WORKS OF HIERONYMUS BOSCH

No meadows, no hellish landscapes.
Half-length figures, dramatic
close-ups. In *The Crowning with Thorns*
and in *Carrying of the Cross*,
we are so near the event
we participate in it physically,
psychologically. The symbolism
is complex. The four executioners
might be the four ages of man,
the four temperaments,
the four seasons, or
the four variations of human cruelty.
They also might be four old drunks
from the East Carolina Ice House.

THE ICE HOUSE

The Ice House was founded in 1932, years before the appeal of Prohibition, so business must have been *sub rosa*. It sits on a corner lot on Griswold and Washington, the neighborhood commercial and residential. Mostly white. It is not as popular as the other ice house on West Alabama and Colquitt.

To begin with, it literally was an ice house—a big room storing blocks of ice and ice-cold beer. Customers took the blocks home for their ice boxes. When refrigeration was invented, the ice went, but the name remained the same.

Today it has a half-basketball court, a horseshoe pit, a barbecue pit, a meat smoker, picnic tables and of course a bar—two in fact, one in front, one in back. It serves fifty brands of ice-cold beers, including Lone Star, Shiner, Shiner Bock, Fireman's 4-Blonde Ale, St. Arnolds' Summer Ale, and Stella Artois. The most popular beer is Budweiser Light, and Friday nights there is live country-western music, like the New Age Birth Band. They serve hot dogs on Friday nights to compete with the West Alabama Ice House. Half the patrons these days seem to be named Jason. They call one "Jason Number Eighteen." Parking is at a premium, and the residential neighbors object to all the cars and especially to the noise and loud music. So far they've been unable to do anything about it.

Over the door of the Ice House is a sign:

BEER—HELPING UGLY PEOPLE
HAVE GREAT SEX SINCE 1862

Over the latrine in the men's room is another sign:

WE AIM TO PLEASE.
YOU AIM TOO, PLEASE

Other signs:

IF YOU'RE HERE TO FORGET,
PLEASE PAY IN ADVANCE

BEER: HELPING WHITE GUYS DANCE
SINCE 1842

MILK SUCKS. GET BEER

THE BEATINGS WILL CONTINUE
UNTIL MORALE IMPROVES

The manager and main bartender's name is Dennis.

THE PROFESSOR

That's what they call him, The Professor. Because he teaches at one of the local universities. Every day at noon he comes in for a glass or two of wine, never beer. Every day he plunks down a book on the bar, reads until it is time to teach. He reads books none of the others have heard of—writers with names like Catullus (which they pronounce Cat-a-lus), Lucretius, Junvenal. ("Hey, he's a juvenile delinquent," one wag quipped.) He wears a nice tweed jacket and bow ties, despite the heat, quite the opposite from the usual denizens in denim.

"Why do you wear ties and jackets?" one asked.

"Because if I can't get their respect one way, I'll get it another."

He always sits in the front, never with the boys in the back. Asked why such a learned gentleman would come to the Ice House every day, he looks over his glass and says softly, "Because the wine is inexpensive and my wife is impossible."

KARL AND THE PROFESSOR

Young Karl begins to hang out with The Professor. "I understand you're a philosophy professor at the university."

"On a good day."

"I read your book on the Philosophy-Kings. It's a kick-ass book."

The Professor never thinks of himself as a kick-ass anything, but he lets it pass.

"I'm a writer too. If I may, I'll bring you a few things."

And so it commences. The Professor is impressed with the boy's papers. Every day they talk philosophy. Every day they have drinks together—wine for the Professor, beers for the young man. The Professor always pays. It is clear Karl is unemployed. The Professor doesn't even know if he's qualified for a job. He never attended college. All his knowledge is self-taught.

Then one day Karl drops his bombshell. "I'm hoping you'll help me out. I'm two months behind on my rent. I need six-hundred dollars, or they're going to evict me on Friday."

"You've mentioned your mother. Can't she help you out?"

"Naw, she's written me off. Says all I do is sit on my ass in that apartment and write. That and go to the library."

The Professor does not want to be put in this

position. There's no way he can be paid back, and there may be no end to Karl's requests. He isn't even looking for a job.

"I'm sorry, I just can't do it." He pays the tab and leaves.

In the weeks to come, word filters back to the Ice House. When the Constable came to evict him, Karl resisted, made a grandstand on the state of writers in America. He tangled with the police, ending up in jail. When released, he found all his things in the apartment house yard. Some of his clothes were in a cardboard box, some presumably stolen. His books and stereo had been rained on and ruined. He ended up living on the street.

All of which makes The Professor feel pretty rotten.

PARKING LOT

One day The Professor arrives for his usual wine, and finds the parking lot is filled with cars. He wonders if someone is holding a party. There are so many cars, there's no room for his in the lot. He has to park across the street, by the convenience store.

Yet when he enters the bar, there is hardly anyone there. He pokes his head out back, and it's the same scene—just a handful of regulars.

"Where is everybody?" he asked Dennis.

"What do you mean?"

"There are all these cars in the lot, but hardly anyone here."

"Oh, that. Those are the cars of the people who got too drunk last night to drive home. They'll eventually come and get them." With that Dennis continues to wash glasses.

BLABBERMOUTH

His name is Arthur, but they call him Blabber-mouth, because he never says anything. He sits alone, never mixing with the good old boys in the back, or the younger men and women in the front. He simply sits and nurses his Miller Lite. No one has ever seen him with a girl. He is a plain young man, large, with a very large nose.

But one day he comes to the Ice House with a girl. Not a great beauty, but attractive enough. They sit together at the bar, and to everyone's surprise, he is talking to her. And not just a little. He talks to her a lot. Her name is Isabel: "Isn't it a beautiful day, Isabel?" he'd ask. She agreed, and then he kissed her. "I love you Isabel," he says. All his timidity and loneliness seem to have vanished.

Every time he returns, they return together. The regulars are pleased to see Blabbermouth almost live up to his nickname. Then one day a young woman comes in and seeing the couple at the bar, rushes over and puts her hand around Isabel. "Why, Helen, I haven't seen you in ages! Where have you been?"

Dennis, who'd observed the encounter from behind the bar, says, "That's not Helen. That's Isabel. She's a regular here."

"It certainly is Helen. I've known her for years. She's Arthur's sister."

HITCHENS

Unemployed old man Hitchens got evicted, and he had no money and nowhere to go. So he started sleeping behind the Ice House comfort stations. He'd show up at the bar in the mornings to cadge a cup of coffee or a beer, maybe a donut if anybody had ordered any.

After the third or fourth morning when he showed up unshaven and wearing the same ugly purple and orange Hooter's T-shirt, Dennis said, "You're not going home at night, are you?"

"Sure I am," Hitchens said.

"Then why are you wearing that same T-shirt three or four days in a row?"

"Shit," Hitchens said. "I got me a drawer full of these shirts—all alike. I likes 'em." And he plucked the Hooter's shirt front proudly.

KARL AND THE PROFESSOR (AGAIN)

One day The Professor opens up his bank account statement and finds his debit account is $1400 overdrawn.

He immediately knows this must be some error, because he rarely touches that account. It's there in case of an emergency.

He goes to the bank and speaks with his personal banker, a brisk, buttoned-up middle-aged lady in a flowered Lily Pulitzer dress. She produces his Account Transaction History. There are many withdrawals, usually in amounts of $20 to $200 dollars. They all had been made in the months of April and May. Most were made at the telemachines at fast-food restaurants on West Alabama, South Shepherd, and Shepherd Square. Sometimes there were as many as five withdrawals a day.

"I never go to fast food restaurants," he tells the banker

"Then what is all this?" she asks, pointing to the spreadsheets.

"Fraud," he says. At which point he takes out his wallet and searches for his bank card. It isn't there.

There is no question he suspects Karl. Karl is the only person who could have had access to the card. The Professor had let him stay over a few nights in April, after he had been evicted from his apartment and said he had nowhere to go. It was a rainy April, and Karl told him he'd been sleeping in the park. The Professor took pity on him. But Karl was The Professor's only acquaintance who was chronically out of money. And Karl is addicted to fast food.

The banker asks him if he has a suspect, and he says he does. He fills out an Unauthorized Debit Card Transaction Dispute Declaration, naming Karl as the probable culprit. He was unable to list a current address for Karl. The public park?

Karl does not phone him, or show up at the Ice House, which confirms The Professor's suspicions. Less than three weeks later, Karl is apprehended at a Starbuck's. There was some altercation, and the police were called. The Professor's credit card was in Karl's possession—along with many others. In fact, the policeman who called The Professor said Karl had a bag stuffed with other people's credit cards. Stuffed!

Karl is now in jail. The Professor broods on his own misplaced trust. The policeman tells The Professor that Karl constantly is railing about how everyone always has been against him—his parents, the police, the city, the state, the Federal Government, and yes, The Professor.

MARI

Her real name is Mary Louise Heffelfinger. That was too long for a marquee, and Heffelfinger was impossible. (Her dear husband used to tease her by saying "Heffelfinger is better than no finger at all...") so she used the stage name Mari Heffel. It could have been better, it could have been worse. An agent told her she had to change her name, and that's what she settled on.

Mari had a nice little career acting off-Broadway. She never made the big time, but she worked rather steadily, considering the insecurities of the profession. Her biggest roles came when she played the stripper in *Gypsy* and the middle-aged Jewish hausefrau in Isherwood's *I am a Camera*. Talk about range! Her favorite lyric was when the stripper sings, "If you're gonna bump it, bump it with a trumpet..." and the trumpet player goes wild in the pit.

She never made it in the movies. Not even bit parts. That would mean moving to Hollywood. To say her career was off-Broadway is to put it mildly. It took her to theatres in Buffalo, Akron, Wilmington and once in Houston. And that is where she met her husband. After her opening night, someone gave her a big party in River Oaks, and there he was: overweight, still handsome, and with a constant martini glass in his hand. He was thrilled, he said, to meet "a star," and a month later they were married. She was his trophy girl. He loved to play with her breasts.

Three months later she found him dead, face down on the kitchen floor in a sea of saliva, a heart attack. She found herself rich and the owner of a big house and two cars.

Theatrical opportunities in Houston weren't impossible, but they nevertheless were limited. She spent hours sending out resumes. She spent nights lying in her big four-poster bed, missing her husband. A passionate longing took hold of her. In the night she would hug her pillow and mutter, "It just isn't fair. Why am I left alone this way?" The few times she went out to parties, men left her alone. Was it because of her money? Was it because she was a recent widow? Was it because she was no longer young?

One day, on a whim, driving on the way back from the Fiesta supermarket, she pulled into the Ice House. She ordered a dry vodka martini on the rocks, only to be told by Dennis they don't sell "that kind of stuff." Only beer and wine. She ordered a glass of dry white wine and looked around.

She saw her, an extremely attractive young brunette, drinking alone. She was smoking French cigarettes, which Mari thought sexy. Mari took her glass to that side of the bar and asked, "Mind if I join you?"

"No problem," the woman said.

"You come here often?" Mari said, then felt like an idiot—the most-used come-on phrase in the world.

"Yah. And you?"

"First time."

And so began a conversation. When the brunette excused herself to go to the Ladies' room, Mari waited a few minutes, then followed her in. Without stopping to think about it, she opened her blouse wide and displayed her breasts.

"What are you doing?" the girl cried. "I'm going to report you to the manager. You're some kind of degenerate!"

"Don't report me, " Mari begged, buttoning up. "I

don't know what came over me." And at that moment she knew if she wasn't careful in the future, she might do something very bad.

SOPHIE

After she gets a little loaded, Sophie tells this on herself:

There's this local liquor store owner who is notoriously stingy. It's said he's so tight, he squeaks when he walks. He underpays his staff. And speaking of staff, he only hires men.

Then one day Sophie goes in his store and asks for a job application. The other clerks stared at her and at the owner. To their surprise he doesn't say there are no openings. He hands her an application.

She quickly fills it out and returns it, which he closely reads. "Fifteen years at Specs?" (Specs is a big liquor store.)

"Yes."

"Why'd you leave?"

"To have a baby."

"And now you're ready to work again?"

"Yes."

The owner sighs and sighs, and keeps staring at her application. Finally he says, "All right, I'll hire you. But on one condition."

"What's that?"

"That you bring your own toilet paper. Everybody knows women use more toilet paper than men."

And she does. Every Monday morning she brings in a new roll and installs it in the employee's john.

When she tells this Sophie laughs and laughs.

The other clerks also laugh and laugh because the brand of the toilet paper is Scott. The owner is such a Scotsman.

DENNIS

"Money doesn't make a scumbag not a scumbag. This is what you get when some college gives a retard an athletic scholarship."

We always wondered where Clancy got all his money. Fancy car, big house. Then one day someone informed the police.

They found twenty dead pit bulls buried in his backyard. He was cleaning up on dog fights.

The FBI has stepped in. He could get a twenty-year sentence for every dog. That's 400 years. I don't think we'll see Clancy in the Ice House anytime soon.

GERTA

One of the regulars tells the tale of his wife, Gerta. She went to a wine-tasting party at the Wyndham-Warwick Hotel downtown. While there someone spiked her glass of wine. She passed out.

When she woke up, she was in bed in a strange bedroom, alone. She had no idea where she was, or when a man might return. She was on the ground floor, so she managed to climb out a window. She found herself wandering alone in the downtown streets at three a.m. She used her cell phone and called her husband. He'd been wondering where in the hell she was, and worried. He got out of bed and drove down to pick her up.

It turns out, after she passed out the manager helped her to his car and took her to his house, which was nearby. Then he left her, because he had to go back to the hotel to clean up after the wine-tasting. When he returned, she was gone.

The question is, who would spike her drink, and why? There might have been a sexual motive—she's very attractive—but no man offered to take her home.

MISS MARY CATHERINE

Then there is Miss Mary Catherine Flood. Homely, with a crooked smile, outgoing, her long grey curly hair always hanging down on each side of her face like cocker spaniel ears. She is not, as they say, "exactly 100 percent." How she started coming to the Ice House is a mystery. Someplace to go to, to get out of the house? She always walks, and she always wears a ratty grey Persian Lamb coat, despite the Houston heat. That coat and Miss Catherine smell musky as an old buffalo in the zoo. (Personal hygiene is not her long suit. Some conjectured she slept in her clothes, perhaps urinated in them.) People try not to sit next to her. Whenever she comes in, there is a rush to other stools. But they are always respectful; always call her Miss Mary Catherine. Her father had been Governor of the state when she was a teenager. It was a job he didn't think much of. He was quoted in the newspaper as saying, "Everybody knows the real power in Texas is the Lieutenant Governor. He's the one who runs everything." As Nelson Rockefeller said, "I never wanted to be the vice president of anything." Governor Flood was a big meaty man with hands like Virginia hams. When he shakes hands at a reception or party, people wince with pain.

Miss Mary Catherine always orders one bottle of root beer, never beer or wine. She pays for it in quarters. She perches on a stool in the front. She tries to make conversation with Dennis or the barmaid or whoever, and when they try to engage her in conversation —politics, baseball—it is obvious she watches no television. She probably doesn't know how to turn one on. Others whisper, "Imagine a world without TV!" She talks about her coming out at the country club. Because of her father's position, she was one of the Junior League girls. They wondered if she was wacko as a teenager, or has it recently happened? One says he'd heard she had a stroke in her thirties.

After her refreshment, she hops off the stool and starts home. If Perfidia were barmaid that day, Miss Mary Catherine would always ask, "Well now, how's your saintly mother?" She knew Perfidia's mother from church. Then she wends her way home in the heat. The assumption is she doesn't have bus money. She lives with her tall, gaunt mother in a big old *Gone With the Wind* house that badly needs painting. No one knows what had happened to the Governor's money. He must have had some, to buy that house, keep her in Junior League, and run for governor.

One day old Mrs. Flood dies. There is a big service at the church. With lots of flowers—it looks like a gangster's funeral. After all, she had been the First Lady of the State. She'd received Christmas cards from the President and proudly showed them. Miss Mary Catherine wears her Persian Lamb and cries and cries. She wets three handkerchiefs.

People wonder what she is going to do, living alone in that big old house. There is no staff. Could she even cook? Could she clean? Someone should at least get her something to do, to take her mind, such as it was, off her grief. It is Perfidia's mother who suggests she be asked to teach Sunday school. It would give her some purpose "Why, she'd be perfect! She has such a childish mind herself, the children will love her." Despite the fact she uses the word "saintly" a lot, the Sunday school stint did not last long. The children held their noses and said she was smelly. The Superintendent observed she could not coherently tell a Bible story. She confused Jonah with David. Said David lived in the belly of a whale after he slew Goliath. Said Pontius was an airline pilot.

One Saturday night Miss Mary Catherine is found by the Constable, walking around the downtown Greyhound Bus Terminal, dressed only in a flimsy nightgown which is in tatters and shockingly transparent. The famous fur coat is nowhere to be seen. "I've got to get back to Austin! It's been so long. They need me to receive at the Rotunda. Daddy always had me in the receiving line. I wore nice dresses, and he always ordered me an orchid corsage." She shook her cocker spaniel ears. Despite the fact she thought she was going to Austin, she had no money, no ticket.

The *Gone With the Wind* house is sold to a young couple, who turn it into a bed and breakfast. On a wrought iron sign out front it proclaims, The Governor's House. Mary Catherine is committed to the State Home for the Feebleminded. That's what they call it, even in the 21st Century. Nobody knows who committed her. It always takes two. Perhaps the Sunday School Superintendent was one, perhaps the Constable. She still wears the coat. She wears it to the breakfast table every morning, even in summer.

CHRIS

Chris, a nice young man locally known for his plumbing jobs, is arrested on his third DWI while driving home from the Ice House late one Saturday night. Because it is his third offense, he is put in jail for eighteen months. It could have been twenty years, but he hired a good lawyer. That cost him five thousand dollars. It also cost him his beloved silver Chevy Impala, which he had to sell to pay the lawyer.

He has three black cellmates, who have no respect for anything or anyone, including themselves. They don't even use deodorant. Somehow they manage to get drugs all the time. Chris doesn't want to think himself prejudiced, but it was hard to live with them in such close quarters. He has nothing to say to them, or they to him. He is a big guy, so he can make it clear there would be no sex between them. At night he hears them doing it, the sounds of sucking.

By day he has to drive a tractor in the fields, in the jungle heat.

One night he is in the dim jail library, avoiding his cellmates, reading a newspaper. He is in despair. He asks himself, Why am I here? Why me? I'm a good guy. Then he turns the newspaper page. There is a story about a DWI who'd just killed a pedestrian in Chris's native city. Then he says, Lord, now I know why I'm here.

When he is released, he never drinks and drives again. He'd drink, but he wouldn't drive. He took an apartment within walking distance of the Ice House.

SALLY

Sally is a beautiful slender blonde. She wears tank tops that show off her tits. No one has ever seen Sally smile. She serves beer looking like the mask of tragedy. She never says hello to anyone.

Dennis, the owner, thinks she's "Awesome," the buzz-word of the year. Everything is awesome, including a pizza. He promoted her to Manager. She manages all the delivery men, including Manny the Masher, the Budweiser guy. She manages the bills and stocks the bar. She manages the mascot Runaway, and Fester the Molester, and she manages Karl the Stalker. She manages Dennis, who took her home after closing time, even though he knew she was a lesbian. He'd never seen her with a guy ever since she began working for him. Maybe that's why she never smiles at any of the men in the bar.

Sally moves in with Dennis. They have an on-again, off-again relationship. She's still the Manager.

NAOMI

Naomi would tell everybody who'd listen: "He started with a single garage sale. He saw the sign, told me he wanted to look around, and parked at the curb. He spent about fifteen minutes looking around, bought a red hot water bottle. That's all.

"Rubber hot water bottle! What'd he need that for in Houston? We've never used it. It's in the bathroom closet somewhere.

"Another day he came home with an old-fashioned hair receiver. I told him I intended to keep my hair in a bob, that I didn't need a hair receiver. He said it was valuable, an antique.

"Before I knew it, he was bringing home junk every day. A broken rocking chair. A matching set of kitchen canisters. A claw-and-ball bathtub. A stuffed moose head. ("Not everybody's got one of those," he said.) A vinyl hassock. A grandfather clock that doesn't work. A ceramic lavabo. Soon the house was filling up with all this stuff. I didn't have room to turn around. I told him he had a sickness. I told him he needed to get some therapy for his buying mania. He wouldn't go see anybody.

"And the worst of it was, he was spending all our money on this junk. When I asked him for grocery money, he'd only give me twenty dollars. Twenty dollars! Finally I just up and left him. I couldn't take it any longer. His sister tells me the house is overflowing now. He's started filling up the garage."

KARL (Yet Again)

Karl sends flowers to each of the four barmaids who work shifts at the Ice House. Each bunch is wrapped in newspapers, tied with duct tape. He has very little money, the flowers look like they were picked from local lawns, which they were.

The four laugh amongst themselves: call him The Stalker. He sits at the bar, picking his nose in public, and wonders why not one of them fell in love with him.

GENE

They call him Gene because all he talks about is his years as drummer with Gene Krupa's Band. "We did all the States, toured Europe, spotlighted Atlantic City and Vegas. Man, it was the life! And Gene, he treated me real good. Gave me solos, even gave me my tuxedo with the silk lapels."

No one asks him why Gene Krupa needed a drummer, when he himself was a drummer. "What happened?" they ask, looking at this aged hippy with an earring and missing teeth. Gene shakes his head.

Dennis gives him the Box Boy job. What the Box Boy does is, he busts down all the cardboard cartons the beer comes in. You'd be surprised how many there are at a place like this. He also cleans the restrooms.

Then one day Dennis catches Gene selling drugs right on the premises. Fires him, tells him never to come back. Every day Gene sits on the curb across the street, wearing a bandana, smoking, drinking convenience store beer. He waves at the Ice House customers as they park. He sorrowfully surveys his lost kingdom.

PUSSYFOOT LACOSTA

With Pussyfoot, you'd assume he got his nickname by being prissy, not walking in a manly manner. Or by being evasive, pussyfooting around issues, rather than being decisive or direct.

Not so. He is a plain man, shy, never married. Before Dennis finds out she is a hooker, and how she earned her nickname of Cherry Pie, Cherry Pie took Pussyfoot back to her apartment one night.

She is not a great beauty, but has nice tits. She makes him put his money (twenty-five dollars) on her bureau in advance. The sheets hadn't been changed in months. They feel like sandpaper.

It isn't a great experience for either. She remarks how tiny his dick is. She says it looks just like a little bunny rabbit. She keeps asking, "Is it in yet?— which is enough to give any man a soft-on.

"You having fun, Bun? My little bunny rabbit?" Then she adds, "I don't feel a fucking thing."

This goes on for some time. Finally exasperated, he takes his bare foot and shoves it up her cunt. She squeals like a stuck pig. Tells him it is the best sex she's ever had—and she's had a lot. She'd make all her other johns give her a foot job.

Somehow word about it got around the Ice House. And that is how he came to be known as Pussyfoot.

MILLIE

One New Year's Eve someone brought two bottles of champagne to the Ice House. Everyone thinks this is great fun—champagne to a beer joint!

Old Millie is quite excited. "Champagne," she coos. "I've never had champagne."

"Then you must have the first glass," is the consensus. They find a clean glass, not a paper cup, and pour. They ceremoniously hand it to her. Then they watch while she takes her first sip of bubbly.

She spits it out. "Tastes just like Alka-Seltzer," she says.

RUNAWAY

Runaway, the brown Ice House hound, is a good dog. Licks hands like lollypops, gives great wag. Called Runaway because he wandered in from nowhere and stayed for fourteen years.

When his back end begins to give out, Dennis takes him to a good vet. Asked by patrons how he was going to pay for it, Dennis says he's my income tax deduction.

You can't do that, they say.

Oh yes I can. He's my alarm system.

Finally one day he has to be put down like a dog. Why do people address a dog with, "Good dog, good dog." And never "Great dog?" Runaway was a great dog.

BERNICE

Bernice worked as a barmaid at the Ice House for sixteen years. She has not had a good life. Her first husband left her. Her second husband committed suicide. She has a son with Down's Syndrome, for whom she hires a babysitter every day. (Some baby—he's in his thirties.) Lost everything she owned in a fire. Luckily the son and sitter escaped. The sitter pulled him out.

She doesn't own a car, rides the bus from the "burbs." She still takes the bus and her luck as her due.

Then one day Dennis decides he needs to up the image of the place. Wants to hire flirty young barmaids who'd please the boys in the back room. (Some boys— their average age must be seventy.) He tells Bernice she is let go with two weeks notice. She shakes her grey pony tail, smiles her yellowed dentured smile. "So much for sixteen years," she says, takes her tips and the bus home.

MARQUEE

Outside the Ice House stands a tall marquee. The kind where you change the letters with a tall pole. You bump the old letters, they fall to the ground. You lift the new letters to make new words.

The announcements vary day to day. Sometimes it's

YOUR EARLY MORNING
DRINKING PLACE!

LORDY, LORDY, LOOK WHO'S FORTY!

or,

SATURDAY NIGHT—
THE BLUEGRASS GIRLS!

Sally told Dennis she wanted to post,

THE ONLY REDNECK DYKE BIKER
BAR IN TOWN.

But he didn't let her do it. It's true they get a lot of bikers on Harleys, a lot of dykes. She pouts for a day, looking more unhappy than usual.

FESTER

Fester sits in back every morning, gossiping with old cronies. He's retired. No beer—he gave up drinking six years ago, when his wife of forty-five years died. (She'd hounded him to abstain for decades.)

Every afternoon he sits in front, harmlessly flirting with pretty young girls. Which is why cronies call him Fester the Child Molester. There are a lot of nicknames at the Ice House. Including Cherry Pie, Pussyfoot, The Stalker, Cooney Houston (because of his bushy black eyebrows), Squeaky Lewis (because of his high voice), Patch Jones (because of his black eye patch), and Pus Smith (You don't want to know why they call him Pus.)

Every night Fester watches the TV at home, ball games if they're on, his wife's photo beside him. He's tempted to drink, but doesn't out of respect.

HELEN

One Saturday afternoon, after the disaster in New Orleans, Dennis wants to take up a collection for the homeless. He appoints Helen, a beautiful blonde, to be the collector.

Helen takes off her blouse and bra and goes around to all the men with a coffee can. In half an hour she collects two hundred dollars.

SALLY (AGAIN)

Sally's girlfriend has become Born Again. She's always talking about Being Saved. About the coming of Armageddon. About being washed in the Blood of the Lamb.

"When she talks like that, I could just bite my tongue," says Sally to Dennis. "And you don't know how serious a thing like that can be to a dyke like me."

PERFIDIA

Pefidia is the only barmaid who is straight, now that Bernice is gone. Dennis hired her because she is beautiful. Long black hair, bright blue eyes. The men call her Perfect Perfidia, not knowing the Latin root of her last name.

In addition to being straight, she is different from the other girls in another way. She comes from a "good," well-to-do family who live in an exclusive neighborhood. She listens to National Public Radio, the others only listen to country-western and hard rock. She raises Siamese cats.

But one thing she has in common with the other barmaids is tattoos. In high school she'd had a rebellious streak, wanted nothing to do with her parents' lifestyle. She did drugs and went out and got herself a series of tattoos. At first they were where he parents couldn't see them—on her lower back, her upper thighs and arms. Eventually she decided, *What the hell?* and got them all over her body. In every color. They began creeping down her arms and legs. Her mother had a conniption fit when she saw them. Her father investigated having them removed, was told it couldn't be done.

Now Perfidia is getting married. She probably wouldn't, except she's pregnant. Her mother insists upon a big church wedding, a catered reception at the country club. They like her fiancé. He's not well-to-do, but he's honest, has talked her out of taking drugs, and he's hard-working, a waiter in a good restaurant in the city, makes good tips.

Perfidia's problem is finding a wedding gown that will cover up all her tattoos. Her mother insists. "You're not coming down the aisle looking like a circus freak!" It's a summer wedding, and all the gowns Perfidia likes have short sleeves and low-cut fronts or backs. She'd better find one soon. That baby's going to start to show.

DENNIS (AGAIN)

Dennis is good looking in a rugged way. His manner is gruff. Many of the female patrons are attracted to him and one of the males, Oliver. Dennis' problems are money and his dick. He's had several wives, and children by all of them. He feels compelled to support them all. And he's always running off to his kids' schools and daycare centers.

The Ice House does well, but Dennis forever is taking money out of the till to support his families and grasping ex-wives. And the place does not run as smoothly as it should if he were around more. Sally is no Manager.

Dennis should have learned to keep it buttoned up.

DONNY

Donny is a big bohunk, looks even taller when he wears his cowboy boots. He is a professional deep-sea diver. He dives mainly for petroleum companies, looking for black gold. He dives as deep as 300 feet. The deeper he dives, the more they pay him.

He is away weeks at a time, and his wife worries a lot. The job is not without peril. Once he was cruised by seven sharks, trying to decide if they wanted him for dinner. They didn't. Once his breathing tube was severed, and he barely made it to the surface.

Ironically, Donny dies in his shower stall at home. He slips and cracks his skull.

RUSTY

"Only friggin' wimps wear helmets."

ROLAND

Roland is probably the biggest bore at the Ice House. There is the (allegedly former) opera singer who regales you with tales of his past triumphs at the Met (though he isn't even lead singer in his church choir.) There is the woman who brings her little white yip-yip dog, and tells you constantly how smart it is. There's the man who loves to cook, and is always passing out recipes. Like one for Crab Après la Chasse (broccoli, onion, mushrooms, garlic, vermicelli, fresh crabmeat), or fiery chicken Vindaloo (don't ask.)

But no one beats Roland. For Roland has a boat. No one has seen it, or knows how grand or modest it may be. But every other word out of his mouth is *my boat*. "I had a great offer for my boat, but refused it, of course." " The kids just love my boat." If anyone says someone missed the boat, he'd jump in and say, "I didn't. Let me tell you about my boat." He'd do it if someone asked him to pass the gravy boat.

Everyone would like to tell Roland to take his boat and shove it up where no sun shines. But no one does. They pretend to have a great interest in …his boat.

STELLA

Stella's husband, Irwin, is always after her to go to the Ice House with him. He calls the place his country club. It's where he goes to relax, chill out, socialize, have a few laughs. Not to mention a few beers. They both are middle-aged with an empty nest.

Lots of guys' wives go with them, he says. Have a ball. There are lots of women there you can talk to. There's Millie—she's a hoot. Helen, she's younger, but you can relate. And Slugger—you could talk clothes with her. She works in ladies' wear at Dillard's. Maybe she can get you a discount.

"I've got enough clothes," she says.

"And the barmaids are nice. Real classy broads."

"I'm not talking to any barmaids," Stella sniffs, patting her blued hair.

"Well you can always talk to Runaway."

"Who in hell is Runaway?"

"The Ice House mascot. A dog."

"I'm not talking to any dogs! What do you think I am, crazy?"

What Irwin doesn't know (she never told him) is that Stella has an aversion to bars. Her parents ran a bar in Dallas when she was little. To save babysitter fees, they'd pack her into the car and take her to the bar, The Dew Drop Inn. They took her crayons and coloring book to amuse her. But Stella was not amused. She heard loud shrieking laughter, saw drunken behavior, even some fist fights. She hated cigarette and cigar smoke, and she hated the loud jukebox, which played the same songs over and over every night. Her coloring book got full, but no one noticed. She hated having to fall asleep in one of the booths before they'd take her home. And there was a man who stood in front of her booth and touched her down there. She was afraid, but she didn't tell.

The memories are still with her. She would never go to the Ice House.

RUNAWAY (AGAIN)

When Dennis finally had to put runaway down after fourteen years (failed kidneys for one thing, he stopped eating for another), Runaway was given a grand funeral.

Because they wanted to notify the patrons of Runaway's passing, the dog was put on ice for twenty-four hours. They put on the marquee,

RUNAWAY 1986-2000

R.I.P.

SERVICE NOON TOMORROW

Dennis and Fester performed the rites. Runaway often spent overnight in Fester's apartment.

Dennis dug the big burial hole, just beside the Ice House, and Fester brought his prized stolen Hilton Hotel blanket to wrap the dog's body. Runaway is wrapped like a mummy in that red acrylic blanket, and lowered to his resting place. Before they cover him up, Dennis throws an empty cardboard six-pack carton in, because Runaway used to parade around the Ice House with one in his mouth, like it was a prize. Then each who attended the ceremony shovels dirt onto the grave. A white wooden cross is put on top.

The mourners return to the bar for a toast to Runaway. "I hope as many people come to my funeral as came to Runaway's," Fester says.

CHARLES

Charles is a tall, heavy-set black man. He is very black, and his manner is intimidating. He earns his livelihood by washing cars at the filling station across from the Ice House. He's so intimidating, when he walks up to you at the bar and insists your car needs washing, you usually fork over thirty dollars for him to wash it, whether you think it needs it or not.

Charles has a mantra, which he repeats at intervals: "I was born here. I'm an American. My parents didn't come here on no boat. They came here on one of the first intercontinental airplane flights. They weren't slaves to the Queen. They worked for the Queen, made wages. They owned their own house. Nobody in my family was ever a slave."

The Professor made a bad mistake with Charles. He went across the street and observed Charles washing his Chevrolet. For thirty dollars he wanted his money's worth. "Why are you being so niggardly with the soap suds?" he asked.

"Nigger?" Charles screamed. "Nobody in my family was ever a nigger! They came here on a plane!"

"It's a Scandinavian word. It means parsimonious," the Professor said.

"Nigger!" Charles repeated. The Professor was lucky he wasn't decked-out. All Charles did was empty the water bucket on the ground, and leave the car full of suds.

THE POET

One regular is known is as The Poet. You'd think that The Professor would be the Ice House Poet, but he's not. He professes, but he doesn't practice.

No, The Poet is another guy. He hasn't published any poems. He simply sits at the bar, and when he has a notion, he writes a poem—always written in black felt-tip-pen, always the length of one of the white bar paper napkins.

Then he ceremoniously presents the napkin to the subject of the poem. Usually the poems are quirky, like the following:

SORRY POEM

I was going to
write you a poem—
then Ned Rorem called,
and I wrote a symphony
instead. I was going to
write you a poem,
then I remembered Arthur Miller
and wrote a best-seller instead.
Because he is dead.
  Keats can rest easily.

RUSTY (AGAIN)

There are many tough customers at the Ice House, but none tougher than the bikers. They come roaring in on their Harley Hogs six at a time, park and rev their engines for a while, just to intimidate. Then they stride up to the bar in their full leathers and helmets, order endless rounds of the cheapest beer. Their language would shock a truck driver. Everything is *fuckin'* this and *fuckin'* that. *Cocksucker. Shitass.*

One of the toughest is Rusty. No one knows what, if anything, he does for a living. He comes in on his bike every day. He has a full red beard, hence his nickname.

If he's one of the toughest, he's also one of the most unlucky. He and his wife each had their own bikes. They were out cruising and pulled into a gas station. A 16-year-old in a truck managed to knock both of them down. The boy had no insurance. She had brain damage, couldn't talk after that. Rusty was in intensive care for months. Neither had been wearing a helmet.

But that's not all. When he was released from the hospital, Rusty became a single biker, and he got hit again, a hit-and-run driver. The driver left him bleeding to death on the pavement next to his trashed-up bike. Before he died a stranger stopped, parked his car, and relieved Rusty of his wallet, wrist watch, and Marine Corps ring. Then he got back into his car and drove away.

RUNAWAY (YET AGAIN)

The Professor loyally wears his gray Ice House T-shirt, with its big photo of Runaway and the headline, HAIR OF THE DOG THAT BIT YOU.

"You know what that shirt means, doncha?" a surly young man asks him one day.

"Of course," says the Professor, in his most pontifical manner. He enjoys nothing more than putting these young whipper-snappers down. "The dog, of course, is Runaway, the late mascot of the Ice House. The phrase, "Hair of the dog that bit you" is a time-honored saying, meaning, "Have some more in the morning to cure your hangover from last night." The Professor felt exuberant.

"That's absolute bullshit! It's referring to the fact that Runaway was vicious, and bit most of the drinkers who tried to pet him. He bit me!"

With that the surly young man turns his back on the Professor.

"I would too," the Professor thinks.

SY

More genial than Roland is Sy. But the maddening thing about Sy is, whenever he sees you he asks the same thing: When did you get out of jail? Then he chuckles mightily. Every day it's the same: When did you get out of jail? Chuckle, chuckle. Variety is not Sy's long suit.

You sure must like saying that, people say.

I do, is the reply. When did *you* get out of jail?

SLUGGER

Middle aged, she is always a fashion plate. Her hair is always colored warm brown and styled. She comes in on her lunch break. She works as a sales clerk at Dillard's.

No one knows how she can afford such beautiful clothes and jewelry on a sales clerk's salary. Even if the store gives her an employee discount, it must still be a lot. Some speculate she is a hooker, but they see no evidence. In the evenings she always leaves alone.

No one knows how she acquired the nickname of Slugger. When asked her name, she always smiles and replies Slugger. No one has seen her driver's license or Social Security card. Maybe her father wanted a baseball player.

She'd have a glass of beer or two, take a peppermint out of her pocket-book (the Ice House isn't the type of place that puts out peppermints), then returns to her job reinforced. She must go without lunch—unless she packs a sandwich and scarfs it down at the store.

One of the most attractive things about her is her sense of mystery. She is very private.

Then Slugger gets ill. She has to have a colostomy. One wag says, "You know what's Slugger's biggest problem now? Finding shoes to match her bag!"

THUNDERSTORMS

And then there is the month of July 2007. There are rounds of thunderstorms every day. Each cool front drifts into the Houston area and triggers additional showers and storms. By mid-month there had been ten inches of rain, with more coming.

Dennis is devastated. People came to the Ice House to sit outside and drink. It was what was unique about the place. But no one wanted to sit outside in a thunderstorm—even under a tent—and risk getting hit by lightning. Day after day the place is near-empty. The barmaids are getting no tips. The box boy has no boxes to bust up. The cartons of beer cans remain in stacks in back. Even most of the hard-core old boys stay away. Finally Dennis has to dismiss the beer delivery trucks. He has no room for more beer, and no money to pay for more. The Budweiser delivery man, Manny the Masher, is astonished.

"It's all this friggin rain" is all Dennis could say. Then he stays inside and watches the Astros game. Fortunately Minute Maid Park has a roof. While he watches TV, Dennis's mind is only half on the game. The other half is dreading telling his mother how far off this month's revenues are.

THE POET (AGAIN)

The Poet hands a white bar napkin to Slugger. The words as usual are in black felt tip pen:

A poem about how glad

We are you're back.
You look fine,
finer than Carolina
in the morning,
brighter than that
Carolina sun.
Keep smiling,
keep slugging, Slugger.

ROLAND (AGAIN)

Trying to get him to talk about something besides his boat, someone asks him what his scariest experience was during his years of international business travel.

"I was in Columbia, outside Bogotá. I was driving a rented Mercedes on this God-forsaken road, when suddenly I saw seven guerillas with rifles blocking the road. I had to stop, of course, I thought they were going to rob me, then hold me hostage. Or kill me.

Roland takes a thoughtful sip of his beer before continuing.

"So what did you do?" we asked, "You're still here. Did you give them the car? Your money?"

"No," he replies. First I threw up—vomit all over the place. I was that scared. Then I shit in my pants— real wet shitty shit which immediately was apparent and stank to high heaven.

"Those big men were so disgusted, they immediately fled. I got back in the car and drove stinkily on.

"It was only that night, in my hotel room, that I realized what a close call that was. What if I couldn't shit?

"Did I ever tell you about my boat?"

BIRD

There is this black bird that starts coming to The Ice House. It flies in with a squawk and lands on the bar. It approaches any drinker who is eating potato chips or popcorn. It is amusing to see it fly away with a big potato chip in its beak.

Only Dennis doesn't think it is amusing. He thinks the bird is a nuisance. His aunt says it is a health hazard. A couple of times he tries to catch it, but the bird is smarter than Dennis.

Then one month the black bird stops coming. It is missed. Did it die? Where do birds go to die? You never see dead birds on the ground.

JEWELL

Maybe because of her name, Jewell, she makes jewelry for a living. But it's not much of a living. She has to buy gold and silver, and that's expensive. But she gets along. She buys her two packs of Luckies a day. Sometimes for months she lives out of her truck, sleeping in the cab, and visiting the Ladies' Room to wash up. They let her park in the Ice House lot for free. Most times everything she owns is in that truck.

Which was the problem. Someone broke into the truck, stole all her jeweler's tools. She had nothing to work with, and no money to replace the tools. If they'd stolen her jewelry, she could make more. But without the tools, she could make nothing.

She tried being a housecleaner but she didn't have the physical strength. She took to hustling for awhile, but her johns complained of heavy tobacco breath.

Then one day in The Ice House she met a prince. Not a real prince, of course, he looked more like a successful toad. He liked her stringy looks (she never ate much), her blonde hair. He didn't even mind her Lucky Strike breath, kissed her right on the mouth.

He took her to Ft. Worth, where he set her up in a jewelry shop of her own. In a fancy mall. People in Ft. Worth had never seen work quite like hers before—intricate animal shapes, unusual floral designs, abstract filigrees.

Last month Jewell returned to The Ice House driving a pink Cadillac. She looked just like a Mary Kay lady.

BLIND-BOY BILLY

Blind-Boy Billy is in his late twenties, with jet-black hair. He doesn't come in every day, only on good days when the sun is shining. He doesn't have a seeing-eye dog. He takes the bus from his apartment, then taps away with a cane from the bus stop to The Ice House. He seems to know when the traffic lights are red and green. He probably goes by the sound of the traffic or lack of it. Strangers always help him cross the street.

He sits outside in the sun with his bottle of Bud Light, face tilted toward the sun like a morning glory. He loves the feel of the sun, and he loves the music on the jukebox. He smiles and smiles when the music is on. It's almost a shit-eating grin. His favorite performer is Billy Joel. He knows how to find the Billy Joel buttons on the juke, and puts his money in and pushes them himself.

People are careful what they say to Billy. Dennis catches himself saying, "Billy, glad to see you!" He realizes he's mentioned seeing.

One afternoon Sally talks to Billy. She asks him if he has a girlfriend. He says No, he used to, but she left him for a sighted person. That's the word she used, *Sighted*. She takes Billy to her apartment. She thinks it's going to be a mercy-fuck. She undresses him like a kid, leads him to her bed.

That night she tells the other barmaids, "Jesus

Christ! It was the best sex I've ever had with a man! And not just because he's hung—and honeys, he is. It's as if God compensated for his blindness. He's got ten inches if he's got one! That boy sure knows how to make love. Maybe it's because he's blind, and has to feel his way around. He knew exactly what to do with his hands and fingers. He sure pushed all my buttons. And that tongue! God Almighty. He told me he was in the band in high school. He could play by ear. He was a trumpet player, and they taught him triple-tonguing. Triple-tonguing! Girls, can you just imagine that?"

Ever since, Blind-Boy Billy is in great demand with the barmaids. Sometimes two of them take him home together. All except Perfidia. She is faithful to her new husband.

TAX LADY

Dennis is behind in his quarterly taxes on the place. Too much child support.

One day a tax collector appears on the premises. She asks for Dennis, but he wasn't there. She asks for a Manager, and Sally appears. The tax collector has the face of a bulldog and the compassion of a great white shark.

She flashes her credentials, then orders Sally to open the cash register. She demands three-hundred dollars.

Putting it in an envelope, then in her brief case, she barks, "Tell your boss he's lucky I didn't clean out the register. Could call it escrow or taxes in advance."

Then she is gone.

Sally is just grateful she is left with enough in the register to make change.

JEWELL (AGAIN)

Two years later Jewell is back, living in a pickup in the Ice House parking lot. She sets up her display on one of the picnic tables. This time the jewelry isn't gold or silver. She is reduced to working with macramé and stones. Pieces sell for around eight dollars.

"How's it going, Jewell?"

"It's a living," she says, then shrugs or laughs. "Well, sort of."

"Whatever happened to the prince?"

"He turned into a toad."

Then one day Dennis tells her she can't spread out her jewelry on the picnic tables. "I'm not turning my bar into a bazaar!" he barks.

JED

Jed tells The Professor that on the way to Los
Angeles, he bought a *Penthouse*. Jed has a face almost
the color of port wine, from decades of hard drinking.
Today's he's sucking on ginger ale.

"You bought a penthouse? If you don't mind my
saying so, I didn't know you had that kind of money."
Jed is a plumber. When The Professor recalls his own
plumbing bills, hundreds of dollars for a clogged drain,
he thinks it is possible Jed bought a penthouse.

"I don't mean the kind you live in. I bought a
Penthouse magazine, to help pass the time on the plane.
Since I stopped drinking, there's not much to do on
those flights. If they show a movie, fine, but it's usually
one I've seen before, or for children. *Lassie Meets
Bambi*, or some such." Jed continues, "So I bought this
Penthouse and took it on the plane, looking forward.
And wouldn't you know it, my seat assignment was
right next to this little old lady dressed all in black.
She wasn't carrying a Bible, but looked like she should
have been. She must have been eighty if she was a day."

"Oh dear."

"Oh dear is right. She even has blue hair. Talk
about stereotypes! I kept that *Penthouse* rolled up for
the longest time, and I was bored out of my gourd. They
didn't show a movie, not even *Bambi*. I almost ordered
a drink, but didn't. Doctor's orders. Finally after two
hours of that, I thought what the hell, and whipped

open the *Penthouse.* I started looking at the pictures, which were bodacious.

"And you know what? It wasn't long before Grandma put on her glasses and was looking over my shoulder at the pictures, too. She seemed to enjoy them, so we ended up sharing the magazine.

"When she deplaned she said 'Thank you for a lovely flight.' And added, 'If you're through with that magazine, I'll take it home.'"

LURCH

One August day Lurch dies. They call him Lurch because he was tall, gangly, and sort of lurched around when he walked. He had large, meaty hands. His hands were what you most noticed about him. You wouldn't want to shake hands with him. Your own would get lost in his.

No one knew his real name, or where he was from, or how he made a living. He was there every day, and paid for his beers with ten-dollar bills. He had a booming voice, and when he greeted acquaintances, it was with a big "Hi, John!" or "Hi, Estella!" He was the kind of guy people call harmless. Of whom it is said he means well. Some kept their distance. They thought he wasn't exactly one-hundred percent. He came and went on a bicycle, which was difficult during the July rains. It was assumed he couldn't afford a car.

Then he fell in the Dixie Queen and cracked his skull on the cement floor. A doctor was called, who pronounced him dead. He said Lurch probably had had a stroke, which caused him to fall.

When a small obituary appeared in the local paper, Dennis cut it out and taped it to the wall behind the bar. He knew it was Lurch because the paper had managed to get a photograph from relatives. Under the photo the paper had printed his real name, Charles Simpson. He originally was from West Virginia, and was forty-nine when he died. What astonished the regulars was, Lurch had been a florist, had had his own business. He sang bass in a local church choir.

"Imagine Lurch being a florist!" it was said.

"Imagine arranging delicate flowers with those hands!"

They realized they didn't know a thing about him, and they'd seen him every day.

DEREK

Everyone considered him a stud. Big, manly, good-looking. Derek was the hot dog boy at The Ice House. They serve hot dogs on Friday nights. The girls adored him. He was good for business, because they bought more hot dogs than normal, just to talk and look at him. He had those smiling Irish eyes.

Derek was so popular, many were surprised when Felicia Phelps announced her engagement to him. She flashed a modest engagement ring. Felicia Phelps? She didn't seem the likeliest of candidates for his hand. Perhaps she had some hidden talents the rest of us were not aware of. Perhaps she gave good head.

They were seen all over town that summer, Felicia and Derek. Seen in restaurants, films, and of course at The Ice House. And then they married. It was a fancy church affair, complete with someone singing "O Promise Me." Perhaps it was her family's money he was after. Her father was the local Ford dealer, and at twenty-three she drove a new Thunderbird.

It lasted less than six months. One doesn't know how word got out about such things—certainly Derek wouldn't tell the tale. It must have been Felicia, being infelicitous with her girl friends. Anyway, the word is that Derek is terrible in bed. Nothing in his pants. This derrick couldn't get it up.

After the split, every time he reports to work he wore this hat with an enormous hot dog on it. It was the largest hot dog you ever saw. He had it made especially. When they call him the hot dog boy, he feigns a modest smile. But those Irish eyes are no longer smiling.

CLINT

Clint always comes in after work wearing his aqua scrubs. He works in a medical center. In late afternoon he is affable, makes the rounds, shakes hands. But people who know him take care. After a few drinks he becomes impossible. No one can disagree with his politics, and after a few beers, he always talks politics. He votes straight Republican, no matter who is running. Anyone who'd vote Democrat is an asshole. He thinks George W. is the best President the country has ever had. George W. should be up there on Mt. Rushmore, and he doesn't want to hear the contrary. When Bush vetoed stem-cell research, Clint bought drinks for the house. He's a lifetime member of the NRA.

Not to be Rebuked

by The Poet

Buzz cut
And brutal
A Feudal lord's attitude
Toward keeping
the proletariat
In their place
His face a hammer
To nail down
Anything sticking up

Abrupt bizarre
Best dealt with
From afar
He likes to get
In your face
His only saving grace
Was working in a caring occupation.

OLIVER

There is this Greek automobile mechanic named Pete. Anyone would admit he is very handsome. Movie star handsome. He doesn't own the shop where he works, he is a nephew. But he is there every day. The owner only looks in occasionally.

An effeminate middle-aged man, Oliver takes his vanilla-colored Mercedes in for a lube job. He gets one look at Pete and is smitten. He makes an appointment for a tune-up that week. Then he brings the car in to be washed. After that he is back for a brake adjustment.

"There's nothing wrong with your brakes," Pete says.

"Oh, I feel them slipping from time to time," Oliver says. This day he is dressed in a purple silk shirt and expensive yellow linen slacks.

"Well, as long as you've nothing to do on the car this afternoon why don't you take time off and have a drink with me. I'll take you to The Ice House."

"Look, you old fag—you're barking up the wrong tree. I'm married. I've got a family. There are cars here that really need fixing, and I need the money. Don't bring your car back any more. You're wasting my time."

"What's wrong with my money?"

"I don't want it."

"Oh, you think you're pretty, don't you? Well, let me tell you, I've seen lots prettier than you!"

Oliver drives directly to The Ice House, where he is

observed weeping over his wine. He's the same customer that has a letch for Dennis. He gets very drunk and the barmaid cuts him off. He has an accident a block away. Then he really does need a mechanic.

SALLY (AGAIN)

Sally comes in one morning with an enormous black eye. Patrons conjecture whether she's gotten it from one of the dyke barmaids, or from rough trade. Most agree it couldn't be from Dennis. He is too much of a gentleman.

The Poet leaves the matter ambiguous when he writes his black-eye napkin poem:

Why?

Easily one
Of the most beautiful women
You would ever see
On a suicide watch
Black eye
A badge of honor
Her entrée into hell
Of her own creation
Her elation
At being brutalized
More satisfying than sex.

CROSSWORDS

Everyday he appears at The Ice House with his crossword puzzle. And it isn't just the local paper, it is the puzzle in the *New York Times*, which reportedly was notoriously difficult. (When the mayor finally completed one, he had it framed and hung it in his office.)

Everyone assumed he is retired—how could he spend every afternoon doing a puzzle?

The others marvel at the speed with which he completes each square. Is he a linguist? A professor? Perhaps even a genius? He is greatly admired. By the time he'd completed two white wines, he lay down his pen with a flourish. He doesn't even use a pencil, so confident he is of his answers.

Then one day, unlike the others, he forgets and leaves the newspaper behind. Curious, Dennis takes it up and examines the puzzle, looking for prodigious knowledge.

What he finds is gibberish. The "puzzle-master" has simply filled in the blanks with nonsense, the very first words that come to his mind. None of them are correct.

When he returns to The Ice House the next day, no one talks to him. No one even looks at him.

After that, he takes his crossword puzzle to the bar across the street. Where he furiously scribbles.

STICK-UP

Three guys, not the color of your dress shirt, if you get my drift, are in the backyard drinking beer. They look nervous, Dennis thinks, he'll keep an eye on them. After a while they move inside to the back room. One of them puts a pistol on the table. No big deal—he just keeps talking to his buddies. This is Texas, everyone has a gun.

But Dennis thinks something is up. He takes his own pistol out of the cash register and tucks it in his pants pocket. As a result, he looks extremely well hung. Oliver should be here.

Soon the boys are holding up patrons in the back room, demanding their cash. In the case of the ladies, their purses. They don't know Dennis is observing all this. Dennis draws his pistol and shoots at the back room ceiling, which isn't a good idea. A shot to the ceiling could ricochet back down and hit one of the customers. He should have shot to the floor. But it is his first stick-up, what does he know?

After that shot, the boys run. They even leave behind their loaded pistols. One went off when it was dropped on the floor. You can see a bullet hole in the bar.

Those boys never came back, and they better not. Dennis has their faces engraved upon his memory. Until now, he thought they all looked alike. And his pistol is still in the cash register.

BLACK DRESS SHOES

He tells this story after a couple of beers. He and his brother returned to their hometown for their father's funeral. At the cemetery his younger brother noticed he was wearing absolutely disreputable-looking shoes. He himself always tried to look stylish.

So the week after the funeral, the older brother receives in the mail a pair of Cole Haan black dress shoes. He'd never heard of Cole Haan, but they look damned expensive. The box included a gift card that says simply, "Enjoy, Bro."

Later that year their mother dies, of a broken heart it is said. The brothers dutifully make the pilgrimage back to the town of Public Landing. He is wearing the same suit, of course. The first thing his brother does is glance down at the other's shoes. It would give him great satisfaction at least to see the new black dress shoes. To his horror, his brother is wearing the old cracked disreputable pair.

"Those new shoes pinched my feet, so I couldn't wear 'em. Gave 'em to the Salvation Army."

That did not help their relations.

BEAUTY

Frances Van was one of the city's great beauties. Even while in high school, you'd see her picture in the papers—she was head majorette for a high school city band, the May Day Queen, and won the title of Miss Bellaire in a beauty contest.

As Miss Bellaire, she won Miss Houston, competing against a dozen other girls. Her mother took her to The Ice House to celebrate. She wasn't of legal age yet, so she sipped ginger ale while her mother had a concoction of cranberry juice and bourbon. The bourbon she had brought in her handbag.

Frances was a natural blonde, blue-eyed, and had a peaches-and cream complexion. Her figure was to die for. She looked great in her white bathing suit and pastel evening gowns. But she had some difficulty with the talent division of the contests. She couldn't sing, couldn't dance, couldn't act. Eventually she settled upon twirling her baton as her talent entry. She bought some fire batons, and the sight of Frances twirling those great balls of fire in her majorette uniform was impressive. She only had one accident. She threw her baton too far and it landed on and ignited the grass skirt of a contestant constumed as a hula dancer.

After the Miss Houston contest, she went on to compete for Miss Texas. Everyone thought from there she'd go on to Atlantic City for the Miss America Pageant. To see her and her mother sitting there in

The Ice House, everyone could see where Frances got her looks. They both had the same profiles, the same eyes, the same blonde hair (however assisted). Except Frances was fresh and exuberant. Her mother looked at life from the edges of a glass of bourbon.

People were shocked when it was announced in the paper that Frances was relinquishing her Miss Houston title, was not going on to Atlantic City. Instead, she was marrying her high school sweetheart, a handsome quarterback named Bo Gallagher.

Everyone assumed she was pregnant. Why else would she give up so much opportunity? Miss America got money, a car, a scholarship, endorsements. The citizens didn't know what-all.

Only she wasn't pregnant. She and Bo didn't have their first child—a girl—until two years after their marriage. They had two more girls in rapid succession. Then the marriage failed. Kaput. Frances took the three children and moved back in with her mother.

They can be seen smoking and drinking at The Ice House every Saturday afternoon, the faded mother and the now faded daughter. Neither are blondes anymore. Both drink bourbon.

Bo Gallaher remarried, a rather plain girl. He coaches junior varsity football. He finally got a son, he says he's very happy.

CLYTIS AND AIR-CONDITIONING

Clytis didn't like his job in New York City anymore. They were demanding too many hours a day. He was even asked to work on the Fourth of July and Thanksgiving. He especially regretted not being able to take his two young boys to the Fourth of July fireworks. Furthermore, lots of younger people, male and female, were after his job. It was only a matter of time. So he sent out some resumes, visited a headhunter.

One contact clicked. It would mean moving to Houston, but what the hell, after all his years in Manhattan, he was sick of the hubbub.

So he told his wife he was taking the family to Houston. A life-long New Yorker, she said, "Like hell you are!"

She resisted for weeks. Time was running out for when he could accept or reject the job. He mounted a monumental campaign to convince her why they should move. He told her it was more money. He told her the boys would go to good free public schools (which they did not in Manhattan). He told her he was sick of his job, wanted to make a fresh start. Finally, he told her he'd be able to spend more time with the family.

Ultimately, it worked ... with a heavy sigh, she said, "All right. I'll move to Houston. But I'll tell you one thing—I'll never use air-conditioning. It's unnatural, it's against nature."

(They lived in the 'burbs on a lake, and never turned the air-conditioning on.)

Clytis made arrangements for electricity and phone to be turned on in the rented house found for them by the company. It wasn't easy. It seems you needed a Texas drivers' license to do anything with anybody. How could he have a Texas drivers' license? He hadn't even moved there yet. Finally he convinced them to let him send them copies of his paid utility and phone bills from New York. Which he did.

They moved on the Fourth of July. When the plane circled Houston, she was amazed. She'd expected a desert, complete with cactus and rolling tumbleweed. Instead it was very green, even in July, with huge old Live Oak trees.

He rented a car at the airport, consulted a map, and proceeded to drive his family to their new home. When he located it, in the outer suburbs, the house of course was dark. His wife looked out the car window at the neighborhood and proclaimed, "I knew it would be bad, but I didn't know how bad. This is a slum!"

It was no slum, of course. The office had sent him Polaroids. The house was cute, and they'd rent there only a year before they bought. He ushered her and the boys and the cat in its carrier out of the car. He discovered a note on the front door:

WE WERE FIXING
TO TURN ON THE ELECTRICITY,
BUT NO ONE WAS HOME.

He found the key in the mailbox, where the realtor agreed to leave it. He'd balked at that, then realized their van would not have arrived, so there was nothing inside to steal. He opened the door.

Inside it was stifling. It was, after all, Fourth of

July in Houston. He rushed to the windows to open them. But this was one of those modern, one-story houses where the windows don't open. The backdoor had a screen, and that was it. The children started crying. There was a built-in window seat with cushions. That's where he installed the children and his wife. He slept in the dining room on the carpeted floor. The carpet was orange, like in an old Howard Johnson's.

The next morning he woke to go to his new office. His razor was electric, so that didn't work. He'd have to shave in the men's room at the office. At least the shower worked. He could get rid of his airport grunge. The stove was electric, so it meant going out for breakfast or catching some cold cuts at a deli. He supposed they brewed coffee at the office.

The office coffee was putrid, and he had a long day. Everyone wanted to "orient" him. The only pleasurable thing was one of the co-workers took him out for a beer afterward. It was a local place called The Ice House. It was cool—open to the elements with picnic tables set all around outside. There was even a breeze, unlike at his house last night. He'd come back, and he did, many nights after work. The beer was cold and the barmaids were hot.

When he got home, and opened the front door, a blast of cold air blew in his face. It was so cold in that house, you could hang meat in it. It was so cold, if they'd had a blanket, the cat would be under it.

"I take it they turned the electricity on," he said to her. He didn't wink, or say anything more about it.

Welcome to Houston.

FINIS

Then one day it is all over. Texaco wants to put up a new service station where The Ice House sits. It's a perfect location for a filling station, they say—busy street, corner lot. They made Dennis' aunt an offer she couldn't refuse. She said she had her old age to think about.

"What will I do?" Dennis asks her.

"Oh, you'll find something," she says vaguely.

The regulars are distraught. If The Ice House had come down for a fast food joint, at least they'd have somewhere to go. But you can't hang around a Texaco station. If you did, you'd probably get arrested.

It only took one day to knock down The Ice House. Some of the regulars watched. Others couldn't bear to see it.

Then one day they dispersed—The Professor, Karl, Blabbermouth, Hitchens, Sophie, Miss Mary Catherine, all the rest. Where did they go? A few took solace in old people's homes. A few took to The Moose. But everyone admitted it wasn't the same. Dennis, still unemployed, has not spoken to his aunt since she announced the sale. She plans to move to Florida.

The Texaco station seems to be thriving. All that remains of The Ice House is Runaway's bones in the ground.

ABOUT THE AUTHOR

Robert Phillips is the author and editor of over thirty books of poetry, fiction, and criticism. His previsou books of fiction include *The Land of Lost Content* (1970), *Public Landing Revisted* (1992), and *News About People You Know* (2002). Phillips lived in and around New York City for thirty years, then moved to Texas to become the Director of Creative Writing at the University of Houston, a position he held for some years and where he taught. His prizes include an Award in Literature from the American Academy of Arts and Letters, a medal in poetry from The Independent Publisher Book Awards, and he is a member of the Texas Institute of Letters.